DOWN THE MEMORY LANE

1988-2018

30 Years of Christ Church Noida

DOWN THE MEMORY LANE

1988-2018

30 Years of Christ Church Noida

Late M.L. Lukose

Anandkumar Peter

Kamna Cowasjee

2019

Down the Memory Lane: *1988-2018–30 Years of Christ Church Noida–* Published by the Rev. Dr. Ashish Amos of the Indian Society for Promoting Christian Knowledge (ISPCK), Post Box 1585, Kashmere Gate, Delhi-110006.

"I will not give sleep to my eyes
Or slumber to my eyelids,
Until I find a place for the LORD,
A dwelling place for the Mighty One of Jacob."
(Psalm 132:4-5)

ISBN: 978-93-88945-46-2

Laser typeset by

ISPCK, Post Box 1585, 1654, Madarsa Road, Kashmere Gate, Delhi-110006 • *Tel:* 23866323

e-mail: ashish@ispck.org.in • ella@ispck.org.in
website: www.ispck.org.in

Dedicated to

Late Col. Lukose – 29th September 1937-23rd January 2019

The authors of this memoir dedicate this work in fond memory of one of its co-authors, Late Col. M. L. Lukose, who initiated this project.

Late Col. Lukose worked relentlessly for a long period of time collating, compiling and verifying historical information and photographs tracing the history of Christ Church, Noida over a period of 30 years. He spoke to people who were present at the time the church was planted. With earnest prayers for the departed soul, we dedicate this book to Col. Lukose.

Contents

Acknowledgements

It is heartening and commendable that just a few months after assuming the pastoral responsibilities of CCN, our Presbyter-in-charge, Rev. Sunil Solomon Ghazan decided to promote the publication of the memories of those people who were associated with CCN for decades. He was inspired by the work done by his precessors.

When such a work is produced after a period of three decades, normally hearsay tends to creep in. However, authors were fortunate to have facts first hand from the founder of CCN, Rev. Col. Lawrence Massey. The authors are grateful to him for recounting events in great details and with accuracy, and in many instances supporting these by carefully preserved documents. He narrated events in its chronological order and the role of people who made it possible without bias or favour. We have, gratefully, recounted his memories and evidence he had carefully archived, as accurately as possible in this book.

Col. M.L. Lukose

The church was planted on the 13th November 1988. Though Col. M. L. Lukose, and family, after retirement, settled in Noida in January 1989, the family joined the church building efforts few years later. After they began worshiping in the Noida CNI church, at some point in the progress of the church, Col. Lukose worked closely with the founder Presbyter, Rev. Col. Lawrence Massey and thereafter with all the presbyters who succeeded Rev. Col. Massey. He had also held important offices as Secretary and Treasurer and shouldered several responsibilities in the church all through the years till the present time, placing him in a position to record his memories accurately, to the best of his knowledge and ability. Col. Lukose recalled with gratitude the fact that his wife Mrs Manorama Lukose has also supported him in all his efforts in the church and enriched this work of his. Col. Lukose recalls that Mrs. Manorama Lukose was a member of the PC by virtue of the fact that she had held the positions of President and Secretary of WFCS for a number of years, and later as a regular member of the PC for a stint of 3 years.

Mrs Kamna Cowasjee

The story of the second co-author, Mrs Kamna Cowasjee, wife of Wing Commander Ransford Cowasjee, (Retd), is almost identical to that of Col. Lukose, except that the Cowasjees took up residence in Noida in May 1989. But in no time they were into active participation in virtually all Church activities, in building a congregation and keeping the church going. Mrs Kamna too benefitted with the family's close association with Rev. Col. Massey and other presbyters who succeeded him. Mrs. Cowasjee was not only responsible for organising the Church Annual Garden Fete but also in bringing out the brochure year after year. She did considerable research into the background of the church for the Silver Jubilee Brochure which she co-edited with Mrs. Roma Naomi Das, another contributing member of

CCN. "Her experience as a PC member in the mid-nineties and later post 2004, and that of her husband Wg.Cdr. Ransford Cowasjee's involvement in the Church construction period and later in various capacities including being a Pastorate Committee member, have all contributed to their first-hand information of Church activities.

Mr Anandkumar Peter

The third author, Mr Anandkumar Peter, has been worshipping in CCN for about 18 years. God has blessed him with multiple talents and placed him in the thick of all spheres of church ministry, be it accounts and finance, administration, conducting of worship services and delivery of sermons, organizing Annual Family Retreats and Workshops, specially supporting Rev. Dr Paul Swarup & Rev. Kamal Mall, and being a resource person whenever called for. He was part of the team led by Rev. Dr. Paul Swarup in the preparation of study materials for the Lent Group studies. He continues to be the Founder Editor of the 'Scroll', our church newsletter. He served two terms of several years as the Treasurer and the modernisation of the church accounts, turning it into a model for church accounts, stands to his credit. His close association with Rev. Dr. Paul Swarup and Rev. Kamal Mall has enabled him to pen, accurate memories of church activities for over 14 years of their tenure.

⚬⚬

Others who contributed in this effort by narrating their firsthand experience of the respective periods and providing documentary evidences of events are Rt. Rev. P. B Santram, Former Bishop of the Diocese of Delhi, CNI, Rev. Col. Lawrence Massey, the Founder Priest, Mr. Rohit David, Vice Admiral H. Johnson, (Retd), Col.

P. D. Shah, (Retd), Mr. Alex John, Mrs. Pramila Lal, Mrs. Shirley Egbert, Brig. Rajiv Williams, (Retd.), and Mrs. Christy Franklin, Administrator of CCN, to name a few. We are grateful to them for their support and valuable contribution.

We are especially thankful to Mr. John Solomon, the Resident Editor of the CCN Newsletter, the 'Scroll', for providing editorial support from time to time.

We are grateful for the good wishes and prayers sent in by our present Bishop of Diocese of Delhi, CNI, Rt. Rev. Warris K. Masih, our Presbyter-in-charge, Rev. Sunil Solomon Ghazan, the founder Presbyter Rev. Col. Lawrence Massey, our past presbyters Rev. Dr. Paul Swarup and Rev. Kamal Mall. We proudly reproduce their messages herein.

Additional note by the co-authors: Just as we were getting ready to pass on the manuscript to the publishers, Col. Lukose passed into glory on the 23rd January 2019. This book is, therefore, dedicated in his found memory.

Preface

This is the success story of a church, planted by a very small group of devout Christians in the newly established town of Noida, an acronym for New Okhla Industrial Development Area, which, in 30 years has achieved enviable wholistic growth and has become a point of reference to other churches. An earnest effort has been made to record the memories of the authors, as one could best recollect, as they were closely associated with Christ Church, Noida (CCN for short), at varying periods, during the 30 years of the existence of the church. We are thankful to God Almighty for his immense blessings upon us and for safely bringing us to this point in time and inspiring us to write down our memories. We have not been alone in this effort, many other members of CCN pitched in with their personal memories, most of which have been incorporated at appropriate places in this book.

A repository of memories of any organisation is the sum total of the memories of the individual members at any point in time. Since people move on for various reasons, this repository becomes dynamically variant. Therefore, having seen and experienced the growth of CCN, and having been active participants in the life and ministry of the church, we felt it would be appropriate, for the benefit of the present and future generation of faithful, to record important events through the years and the contribution of various people who made it possible. Not only did CCN develop spiritually, but it also did not lose time to accept its social responsibilities and began to look outward through various outreach projects.

During these thirty years, CCN has been pastored, beginning with its founding priest, Rev. Col. Lawrence Massey, who was inspired by a compelling vision to plant this church, followed by Rev. Dr. Paul Swarup, Rev. Kamal Mall and now Rev. Sunil Solomon Ghazan. During this period the congregation has grown from a few initial believers to a strength of over 200 dedicated families comprising about 600 individual members. Therefore, this book is structured according to the timelines of its presbyters.

CCN has a great address, being situated in the heart of Noida. Its central location, RC-1, Sector- 29, in the vicinity of Botanical Garden Metro Station is an added advantage in terms of visibility and accessibility. CCN has become an enviable role model in the Diocese of Delhi, proudly propagating "Unity, Witness and Service", the motto of CNI.

Finally, as the writing is done from our memories and some records in our personal possessions, we accept that there could be several omissions and commissions, which if brought to our attention will be remedied in the next edition of this 'Memoir' if that is the will of our Lord Jesus Christ.

Rev. Sunil Solomon Ghazan
Col. M. L. Lukose
Mr. Anandkumar Peter
Mrs. Kamna Cowasjee

Preface

Greetings

October 31st, 2018

Greetings from the Diocese of Delhi and on my personal behalf, in the mighty & precious name of our Lord and Saviour Jesus Christ.

I am glad to know that Christ Church, Noida is celebrating its 30th anniversary on 13th November 2018. I am pleased to note that to mark the occasion they are releasing a History book which records the contribution made by their pastors, stalwarts, founding members and other members of the Congregation.

Remembering one's roots helps one retain humility and realize God's mighty hand in everything that happened to make Christ Church, Noida what it is today.

Hence, such documents are significant in their own way and essential for reference, on various issues related to the past, so that justice is done to all who otherwise could be forgotten in course of time.

On this auspicious occasion, I send greetings and hearty congratulations to the Presbyter, Rev. Sunil S. Ghazan for this initiative, all members of the Pastorate Committee and the CCN congregation at large.

I earnestly pray that God would continue to bless and use you to remain powerful witnesses for the resurrected Christ.

Yours in His Service

The Rt. Rev. Warris K. Masih,
Bishop of Delhi, CNI

☙❧

I am grateful to God for his continued mercies upon us, as members of the Christ Church Noida family.

I remain indebted to my predecessors, namely Founder Presbyter, Rev.(Col.) Lawrence Massey (November1988-2004); Rev. Dr. Paul Swarup (2004-2011); Rev. Kamal Mall (2011-2018) whose hard work and dedication have made the Church what it is today. I have taken over from them from 17th June 2018.

It is important and biblical to remember one's roots; as it is written: "Beware that you do not forget the Lord your God by not keeping his commandments, his judgments and his statutes which I command you today...then you say in your heart, 'My power and the might of my hand have gained me this wealth.' And you shall remember the Lord your God, for it is he who gives you the power to get wealth, that he may establish his covenant which he swore to your fathers, as it is this day." Deuteronomy 8:11, 17-18.

The very idea of compiling 30 years memory is this, that the CCN members, (founding and present) remember their roots with humility, awe and fear of God, don't say in their hearts that it is by the power and might of their own hands have they gained all this. That instead they may acknowledge, that it is the Lord their God who gave them the power to get wealth.

My slot of contribution is recorded by the history writers of the Church namely Col. Lukose, Mr. Anand Peters and Mrs. Kamna Cowasjee and others who worked behind the scenes to produce this compiled 30 years memories, of this very young Congregation, may it help them look back at the contribution of their Shepherds whom God sent and appointed to serve him and his people.

May God bless the Christ Church Noida for many more years to come!

Yours in God's service,

Rev. Sunil Solomon Ghazan

C33&80;

November 12th, 2018

It is my great joy and privilege to wish members of Christ Church Noida, the Lord's abundant and rich blessing on the 30th-anniversary celebration of the Church.

God has always blessed this Church, and will continue to do so. Remember what St. Paul said to the Philippians, "My God shall supply all your needs according to his riches in glory by Christ Jesus(Phil 4:19). When our central focus is on Jesus, he will provide all our needs and growth for the Church.

When we put God's word in our mouth and rely on his promises in our lives, commitments and plans, we will see wonderful things happening. Let us conclude with Phil. 4:29 which says" Let no corrupt communication proceed out of your mouth but that which is good to the use of edifying that it may minister grace unto the hearers."

May God continue to bless Christ Church, Noida.

Yours in Christ,

Rev. Col. Lawrence Massey

ॐ

November 13th, 2018

First of all, I want to congratulate the Rev Sunil Ghazan, the Pastorate Committee and all the members of Christ Church, Noida as they celebrate their 30th anniversary this year. It was a privilege for me to serve this Church,along with Nina and Daniel from 2004 to 2011. When we were transferred from St. James Church it did not have a parsonage. There was an old temporary church where the present parsonage stands. Slowly but surely, we shared with the congregation the vision of building a parsonage. We also suggested that we hold a Fete in order to raise the needed money for building the parsonage. This was done and slowly the work began on the parsonage. We moved into the parsonage in January 2006. This was followed by the building of the parish hall which was also a long-standing need. We praise God for all his mercies in providing for all the need of the Church during this building project.

On the spiritual front, we started to have regular Wednesday evening prayer cells. This was indeed the highlight of the week as we saw God doing his mighty miracles in releasing people who were demon-possessed as well as many who had diseases were healed. Wednesday evening prayers were the powerhouse for the church and all its activities. Along with this we also had the 24 hours chain prayer. Prayer points were shared with members of the congregation and asked to pray for one hour in their homes. This also helped in bringing revival in the Church. Sunday School met during the service and the Youth group met for Bible studies regularly.

One of the things that we introduced was the zone wise Bible studies. We had divided the church into different zones and there were leaders assigned to lead the Bible studies. There was a leader's guide and a study guide which we had prepared and these would be discussed in the various Bible study groups. We did a particular series on studying the Holy Spirit which in the end became a book which was published in English and in Hindi.

The Vacation Bible School was also introduced during this time and many children from in and around the area participated in this. This was another step in the spiritual journey of the Christ Church.. Family camps were held in Torch Bearer's in Dehradun and many families participated in this and were greatly blessed. One day retreats were held on August 15th and January 26th to strengthen the spiritual life of the parishioners.

More than anything else we were nurtured by the love of the members of the Church,who showered their love on us and made us always welcome. We finally bid farewell to Christ Church, Noida in April 2011. We once again wish Christ Church, Noida wonderful and Holy Spirit filled years ahead.

With every blessing, Salom!

Paul Swarup

⊂Ʒ℘⊃

October 31st, 2018

Dear Rev. Ghazan and the congregation at Noida,

Greetings in the Mighty and Awesome Name of our Lord and Saviour Jesus Christ!

Truly, our God is a great God who continues to remain faithful. First, let me congratulate you as Christ Church Noida turns 30 this year. Secondly, I'd like to say that it has been an honour to work in Christ Church Noida for 7 years and that I've been blessed in every possible way while participating in its ministry.

I would also like to use this opportunity to thank God for the ministry of this Church which is so strategically situated. CCN Ministry continues to seek to be a resource to many in the neighbourhood and to the Christian community in this area at large. My prayer is that this ministry becomes a catalyst for the building of healthy local ministries first, which will, in turn, lead to a strong ministry regionally.

As we continue to press along, in years we're hoping to see a revamped Christ Church that we're looking to expand to become "Missionary Church." I look forward to great days ahead as the Holy Spirit leads and guides CCN into the higher heights, and deeper depths in him. God bless you all!

In service to both King and Kingdom,

Rev. Kamal Mall

The Church of North India's congregation at Noida which began with a small group of committed Christians in mid-eighties, meeting for fellowship, and worship in homes of members, has now grown into a large full-fledged pastorate of the Diocese of Delhi. This has happened because of the dedicated and enthusiastic ministry of laypersons and their presbyter-in-charge, the Revd. Col. Lawrence Massey. This deserves encouragement from the wider family of the Diocese of Delhi.

About 8 years ago a large plot of land was procured by Delhi Diocese at Noida for construction of a place of worship and a community for social, charitable and cultural activities. For the past seven years serious efforts have been made to achieve that goal. With intense local initiative and support of the Diocese and many friends of the pastorate of Christ Church, Noida, first a temporary small building for worship was constructed, which was subsequently enlarged. At present the proposed, planned building of Christ Church is almost complete, as part of the first phase of an ambitious plan which includes a community centre and a Parsonage.

I am happy that the pastorate of Christ Church, Noida, are organising a Fete to raise funds to first complete the new Church building and later fulfil their vision of a lively centre of worship and social, cultural and charitable programmes of the Church.

I urge all congregations of the Diocese to generously support this venture, and I pray for God's blessing on the Fete.

Bishop Pritam B. Santram
Bishop of Delhi

Dear Members of Christ Church Noida

I am very pleased that you are making a united effort to build your Church in Noida, you are amongst the very few congregations who have taken up this challenge seriously. I am sure you will be abundantly blessed and Christ Church Noida will become a place of devotion and inspiration not only for you but for generations to come.

May God bless each of you.

Bishop Maqbul Caleb

"*Christ Church Noida wishes to acknowledge the contribution of Bishop Caleb in the very formation of this Church.*

Thank you Bishop for being our guide & mentor"

The Genesis

Rev. Col. Lawrence Massey, on retirement from the Defence Services, with his wife Khurshid, daughter Chitra and sons Austin and Basil, (now retired from the Indian Army), settled in their apartment in Sector 29, Noida in December 1987. Almighty God bestowed upon him a grand vision. He had acquired the Bachelor of Divinity degree, while in active Army Service and was ordained as a Priest, by the Bishop of Nasik, CNI, before he moved into Noida. Since there was no CNI Church in and around the place, he diligently started looking for Christian families, settled there, a town which itself was at the initial period of its development. As per the advice of Rt. Rev. W.D. Simon, Bishop of Diocese of Agra, CNI, whom he met at Agra on the 5th January 1988, he approached Rt. Rev. Maqbool Caleb, the then Bishop of the Diocese of Delhi, CNI on 18 January 1988. Having been convinced of the spiritual needs of Christians in Noida, he gladly supported Rev. Col. Lawrence Massey and encouraged him to establish a CNI Church, in the National Capital Region (NCR). He was advised by the Bishop, to look for a plot of land for a church building.

Subsequently, after receiving a written request, from 12 Christian families living in Noida, on 1st October 1988, Rt. Rev. Maqbul Caleb, appointed Rev. Col. Lawrence Massey, as the Honorary Presbyter-in-charge of the CNI Church, Noida, vide his letter No. Clergy-A/72/88 of 1st October 1988. Those who signed this pioneering document were Mr. C.M. Dina Nath, Mr. I.N. Egbert, Capt. J.A. Peters, (Retd.), Mrs. F.C. Gergan, Mrs. D. Tressler, Mrs. Lilly R, Maj. Gen. RS Diol, Mrs. Ruby Santram, Mr. Sittan Lal, Wg. Cdr. SK Tressler, Mrs. Venita Massey and Wg. Cdr. Asa Michigan.

1988 — 2004

First Divine Service

Little over a month after the installation of Rev. Col. Lawrence Massey, as the Honorary Presbyter, for the church, on Sunday, 13th November 1988, Bishop Rt. Rev. Maqbul Caleb, assisted by Rev. Col. Lawrence Massey, conducted the 1st 'Divine Worship and Holy Eucharist Service' at Rev. Col. Lawrence Massey's residence. The seed was thus sown and the faithful, including retired Defence Services veterans living in Noida, attended the First Service of the Lord's Supper. Thereafter, worship services were regularly held on Sundays, in the houses of the faithful, on rotar, for about three years.

Home Church

Sunday Services were conducted, from 1988 to 1991, in the homes of, Sector 21, Mr. Rohit David Wg. Cdr. R A Cowasjee, Cdr. N. A. Mullerworth, MWO Solomon; (Sector 26) Mr. I. N. Egbert, C.M. Dinanath, Alex John; (Sector 28) Wg. Cdr. Dennis Harrison, Gen. Eric G. Kerr, (Sector 29) Col. Raman, Rev. Col. Lawrence Massey, Capt. John Peters; Sector 37: Col. P. Dyes, Mr. Anil Santram, Maj. Gen R.S Diol, and Col. John Tressler.

Pioneers

Enquiries made to few initial members and looking at the available records reveal that following devout Christians attended the First Service of the CNI Church:

Mrs. Jane Maqbul Caleb, Mrs. Khurshid Lawrence Massey, Mr. Rohit David and Mrs. Reeta David with their 2 children, Mr. Anil Santram (Late) and Mrs. Shunila Santram, Capt. John Peters, (Retd) and wife Renu, Mr. C. M. Dina Nath (Late) and wife, Mrs. Reeta Dina Nath (Late), Mr. I. N. Egbert (Late) and Mrs. Shirley Egbert with their 2 children, Mrs. Dorothy Tressler, Mr. Alex John and Mrs. Kiran John with their son Vikram, and Wg. Cdr. Sushil Tressler (Late) and wife Mrs. Mrinalini Tressler.

Formation of the Ad-hoc Pastorate Committee

As advised by Bishop Maqbul Caleb, an Ad-hoc Pastorate Committee, to hold office till the first Annual General Body Meeting, was formed, in a meeting held, on the 20th Nov 1988, presided over by Rev. Col. Lawrence Massey, after the Service, at the house of late Mr. Anil Santram. Late Cdr. N.A. Mullerworth, Mr. Anil Santram (Honorary Secretary), Mr. Rohit David (Honorary Treasurer), late Mr. CM Dina Nath, Mrs. Sheela Bhalla, and Mrs. Khurshid Massey were elected as the members of this first Pastorate Committee. Mr. Alex John was nominated as a Committee Member in waiting. Mrs. Shunila Santram was co-opted for Sunday School and as an ex-officio member of Pastorate Committee.

As decided in the meeting, a Bank Account, in the name of 'CNI Church, Noida' was also opened.

First AGM and
Formation of the Pastorate Committee

Subsequently, in 1989 or 1990, the first AGM was held. The AGM formally elected Cdr. Neville Mullerworth, (Retd.), Mrs. Helen Harrison, Mr. Rohit David, Mr. Alex John, Capt. JA Peters, (Retd.) Col. P. Dyes and Mr. Anil Santram as members of the first Pastorate Committee.

First Baptism and Confirmation

During the initial period of 3 years of home worship, the church considered and conducted Baptisms and Confirmations of Youth.. Record shows that the first person to be baptised was Alexander Massey, son of Capt. Austin Massey and Mrs. Nisha on the 19th February 1989. Alexander now is a smart, young Major in one of the Elite Corps of the Indian Army. Record also shows that in the Confirmation Service held in the house of Mr. C.M. Dinanath with Rt. Rev. P.B. Santram, then Bishop of Diocese of Delhi and Rev. Col. Lawrence Massey as celebrants, Ms. Ambika Nath daughter of Mr. CM Dina Nath and Mr. Rajiv Egbert, son of Mr. Egbert were confirmed on 27th May 1990.

Women's Fellowship

With the vision to provide Christian service, the Women's Fellowship (WFCS), under the leadership of Late Mrs. Georgina Kerr, was formed in 1992. Late Ms. Usha Shukla, and late Ms. Rosalyn Nair, (in addition to her part-time duties as the first Accountant-cum-Administrator of the Church), were nominated as office bearers by the women of the Church. Subsequently, President, Secretary and Treasurer were elected during the Annual General Body Meetings of the WFCS.

Mrs. Usha Shukla, Mrs. Helen Harrison, Mrs. Usha Dyes, were some who served as its President for many of the founding years with Mrs. Kamna Cowasjee as its Secretary and Rosalind Nair and later, during the tenure of Rev. Dr. Paul Swarup, Ms. Shiela Solomon became its Treasurers. Mrs. Manorama Lukose and Mrs. Shanon Mukha, Late Mrs. Lilly Abraham, Mrs. Leena Nambiar served the WFCS as some of its presidents, while, Mrs. Shirley Ramsey and Mrs. Uma Stephen were Secretary and Treasurer respectively.

Outreach Activities of WFCS

The sick and those in distress were visited and prayers and any kind of assistance were rendered to nearby poor homes. Some of the homes visited by the WFCS were St Mary's Old Age Home, Grace Home, Najafgarh Old Age Home, Love India (Girls Orphanage, Delhi), etc. An eye operation of an orphan blind girl was financed, monitored and supported, and so was the treatment of a boy with crooked legs until he could walk. They also took an active part in other Christian Services. Since the last few years, CCN WFCS is supporting two girls of St. Michael's Church and orphanage. Support rendered to the Medical Camp organized by the Church during Silver Jubilee celebrations is also commendable.

Our Women members participated in the 'Diocesan Fete' at Cathedral Church (Diocesan Ekta Utsav), with a 'Cake and Brownie Stall', first time in 1989, barely a year after the inception of the Church, (volunteered by the Cowasjees, Harrisons, Alex Johns and Santrams), and it was a remarkable achievement. The WFCS also, participated in the Diocesan WFCS Fete at St. James' Church in1989/ 1990. Entire proceeds of the Ekta Utsav in 1990 was given to CCN towards construction of the Church. Santrams, Alex John family, Shiela Solomon, Cowasjees, Harrison's, assisted by Uma David, Usha Dyes ran the stall till 1997, after which it was handed over to Manorama Lukose, Radhika Judd, Uma Stephen and others.

Participation in the Ekta Utsav is a regular feature, with the addition of a second stall by our Greater Noida congregation (CCGN), WFCS. CCN WFCS is an official wing of the Diocesan WFCS, Delhi. Efforts of Mrs. Lukose, Late Mrs. Lilly Abraham, Late Mr. Vincent Judd and late Mrs. Radhika Judd, Mrs. Shirley Ramsey, Mrs. Leela Nambiar and Mrs. Veena Wesley, Wg. Cdr. Dennis Harrison & Mrs. Helen Harrison, Meshy family, Wg. Cdr. Susheel Tressler, Cdr. N. A. Mullerworth, Grp. Capt. John and Mrs. Usha Shukla, Mr. Anil, Mrs. Jaya Santram, Mrs. Cynthia Duraisamy and Ms. Shunila Santram need special mention. Year after year they made sure that the tradition set years ago by participating in the Ekta Utsav is kept up with great enthusiasm. WFCS helped the church in organising and distributing food on special events. Initially the ladies baked trays of brownies at home while cakes were done at the bakery for Christmas and new years. Love Feast on Maundy Thursdays, Easter eggs and buns for Easter and organised morning breakfast to support their finances.

Allotment of Land

From the Diocesan fund, the Bishop of Diocese of Delhi, Rt. Rev. Maqbul Caleb, as a commitment towards the purchase of a plot in Noida, gave a cheque of 1 lakh in favour of CCN Noida, with the advice to make regular liaison with Noida Authority to make progress towards the allotment of a plot of land. With the blessings of God Almighty a plot of land, measuring 1446 sq. meters were acquired by the Diocesan Society of Diocese of Delhi, CNI, on behalf of the church, in Sector - 29 Noida. This plot was taken over on the 20[th]February 1990, from Noida Authority, after sustained liaison work done by Mr. Rohit David. The allotted plot was a corner plot with roads on two sides, with an irregular trapeziform shape. It had a waste-water drain (nullah) on the rear side. Therefore, 'the plot did not look too good', as opined by Lt. Gen. Eric G. Kerr, one of the founding members, in his memoir. However, the church members were happy and thanked God for blessing the church with this plot of land.

Members during the Initial Period

By November 1993, Deena Nath & Ruth, Solomon, Victor Bendix, Veera Lepcha, Dr. Mathews, Grp. Capt. John F Shukla, Advocate Jai Mangalwadi, Col. Rajan, Lt. Col. Victor Duraisami and Brig. Rajiv Williams and Vineeta Williams joined the Church and all of them jointly gave a further momentum towards Church development. The above names feature in the list of members created by Rev. Dr. Paul Swarup after he took over in 2004, details of which can be found in the relevant period.

In order to do justice to all those whom we could collectively recall having been with the church at the initial periods their names are listed here, alphabetically with a disclaimer that the contributors, have done their best to be as accurate as possible, there can be errors, omissions and commissions in the list that follows:

- Ms. Shiela Bhalla

- Mr Victor Bendix,

- Wg. Cdr. Ransford & Kamna Cowasjee,

- Mr Rohit David and Reeta,

- Col. and Mrs. Victor Duraisami,

- Maj. Gen. Sunny & Shiela Diol,

- Col. Percy Dyes and wife Usha,

- Mr. Vincent Judd and wife Radhika,
- Mr I.N. Egbert and wife Shirley,
- Wg. Cdr Dennis & Helen Harrison,
- Mr Alex & Kiran John,
- Lt. Gen. Eric G Kerr Mrs Georgina Kerr,
- Mrs Veera Lepcha,
- Col Lukose & Manorama Lukose,
- Col Lawrence Massey and Khurshid Massey,
- Dr Matthews, Mr Jai Mangalwadi,
- Meshy family,
- Cdr N.A. Mullerworth,
- Mr KG Minocha,
- Ms Rosalind Nair,
- Mr Deena Nath & Ruth Nath,
- Mr CM Dina Nath and Reeta Dinanath,
- Capt. JA Peters & Renu,
- Col Rajan,
- Gp Capt. Shukla and Usha Shukla,
- Ms Ruby Santram, Mr Anil Santram and Shunila Santram,
- Col & Mrs P D Shah,
- Mr & Mrs Solomon,
- Wg. Cdr. Susheel Tressler and Mrs Mrinalini Tressler,
- Col John Tressler & Mrs. Dorothy Tressler,
- Brig Rajiv Williams & Vineeta Williams.

Re-christening of the Church

In 1994, the church otherwise known as CNI Church was re-christened as 'Christ Church', Diocese of Delhi, CNI, at its present location at RC-1, Sector 29, Noida, (UP). Congregants grew to about 35 families consisting of 263 members and 65 communicants by 1994. Two services in the morning, one in English followed by one in Hindi and a Combined Service on the First and Third Sundays were held. Fifth Sundays were reserved for the Youth. Easter Vigil was held before Sunrise on a small hillock in Nandan Kannan Park in sector 15, Noida on the 12th April 1998, for the first time.

Temporary Shed to a Regular Church Building

A small temporary asbestos sheet covered single-brick-wall structure was constructed at the Eastern corner of the land allotted for the church, to accommodate about 25 -30 worshipers. The families pooled in their resources for this temporary construction and dedicated it as a Chapel. Divine service commenced in this Chapel on the 30th May 1991. "Initial possessions in this first chapel were 8 folding steel chairs, 2 wooden benches, a few repaired stools and a table a Coffee Table on a raised platform was used as the Altar", wrote Gen. Kerr.

In 1990, as the number of worshipers increased and the temporary structure in which the worship was being conducted became inadequate to accommodate all, it was further extended. Under the advice and able supervision of Col. S. Rajan, an Army engineer, who also had joined as a member of the church, this was achieved by breaking only the west-sidewall, leaving the main plot for the construction of the permanent church building. An altar under the supervision of Lt. Gen. Eric G. Kerr was made with the wood picked from the home of Col. P.D. Shah, who was getting his house construction for occupation after retirement. "I was proud to go to this Altar", Gen. Kerr stated. (It is in this location the present Multi Utility Complex is located).

The construction of the main building was delayed, and the Church was called upon to pay a fine for this delay to the Noida administration and the extension of the date of construction. One more year passed and the plans for the construction of the Church building were still being discussed and finalized with the new architects, the Methodist Engineering office headed by Mr. Noel Vaghela, a very experienced and able architect, and a specialist in the construction of church buildings.

It was in March 1996, Col. Parvez Shah, (Retd.), permanently settled in his Flat in Noida, Sector 29, after his retirement from the Indian Army, Corps of Engineers. We have drawn upon the memories of Col. Shah, Admiral Johnson and Mr. Alex John for the span of the period from 1996 to 2004, so far as it related to the construction of the main Church building.

After due deliberations, the building plans, initially prepared by Mr. Navin Das, and approved by the Noida Authority, were finalized, in consultation with M/S Methodist Engineering Services by the Pastorate Committee.

Laying of the Foundation Stone of the Main Church

12th November 1995 was the day on which the foundation stone of the Church was laid. On that day, Bishop, Rt. Rev. Pritam B. Santram presented an artefact, a 'gold ringed piece of rock from the tomb of Jesus, embedded in a highly polished marble of the size 2"×2"×1". It was presented to Bishop Santram when he was in England. This was displayed to the congregation, during the worship service on that day and was embedded deep in the plot as the foundation stone, in a ceremony presided by Bishop Santram. The elders and the PC decided that seven specific members should assist Bishop Santram. The younger people among the seven were Ms. Kritika Santram, daughter of Mr. Anil and Sunila Santram and the oldest was Mrs. Milred Clarke. Besides them, Mrs. Kiran Alex John and three others participated.

In remembrance of Jesus Christ pointing to Psalm 118:22, in Matthew 21:42 saying, "Have you never read in the Scriptures: 'The stone which the builders rejected has become the chief cornerstone", on the Easter Sunday the 30th March 1997, according to Mr. Alex John, this artefact was carefully dug out and used as a 'Corner Stone' of the main church building on the altar side wall. This gesture indeed was meaningful and CCN must remember this all the time.

Design and Construction of the Main Building

The construction phase and the related events as narrated by Vice Admiral H. Johnson, Col. P.D. Shah and Mr. Alex John are reproduced here:

Vice Admiral Johnson, recalled the events of this period thus:

"Around that time an Architect named Navin Das who lived in Noida lost his mother. Rev. Col. Massey was very helpful to the family in arranging and executing the last rights of the deceased. As a 'thank you' gesture, Mr. Navin Das offered to design the Church building and oversee its construction. His sister Mrs. Kalyan Masih from Nebraska, USA had come down for her mother's funeral. Being a devout Christian, she offered financial help from her home church in USA. This was gratefully accepted.

I think eventually about Rs 1.2 lakhs was donated by members of Capitol City Church congregation at Nebraska, USA. As we did not have FCRA, the amount was received by us through the Diocese of Delhi, CNI. For personal reasons not known to me, somewhere along the line, the Architect Mr. Navin Das lost interest in overseeing the construction of the church building.

By God's grace, in March 1996, Col. Pervez Shah retired from the Army Corps of Engineers to settle down in Sector 29, Noida. He volunteered to take over planning and supervision of the construction and continued to do so till the main church building was completed. His suggestion to expand the church building and a mezzanine floor to accommodate another 50-70 more worshippers were accepted and incorporated in the plans. Late MWO Solomon was appointed to assist Col. Shah. Besides others who may have helped, the names of Wg. Commander (Rtd) Ransford Cowasjee (who handled the purchases) and Mr. Alex John (now settled in Bengaluru) are worthy of special mention.

The Pastorate Committee officially appointed Col. Parvez Shah (Retd.), as the engineer-in-charge of the project in March 1997. Junior Engineer Mr. Patrick of the Architect M/S Methodist Engineering Services was engaged to assist Col. Parvez Shah on a nominal honorarium of Rs. 3500/- per month. This was in addition to the Architect's fee paid to the firm.

Col. Parvez Shah (Retd.), started working for the new church building. The design, size and actual location of the Church on the allotted irregular shaped plot of land was not very simple and posed considerable technical and legal problems. Here is what Col. Shah had to say about the details of the construction activities:

"The cost estimates made by the architects for Phase-I of the project consisting of main worship hall, electrification and architects' fees worked out to Rs. 12.72 lakhs while there was only Rs. 3.17 lakhs in the building fund account. In addition, Rs. 4-5 lakhs more was required for electric fittings, pews, furnishings, boundary wall with the gate, staircase and other surrounding hard standings.

Financial help to the tune of Rs.1 lakh, towards the construction, was received from the Diocese of Delhi later. The complete onus of financial fulfilment came upon our small congregation consisting of only 49 families.

The drive for funds collection was led and organized by Rev. Col. L. Massey, Vice Admiral H. Johnson, Cdr. N.A. Mullerworth, Mr. K.B. Lal, Wing Cdr. and Mrs. Kamna Cowasjee, Dr. Mathews, Col. and Mrs. Lukose, Maj. Gen. Diol, Mr. Rohit David, and Mr. & Mrs. Alex & Kiran John and was supported by every church member family. Due to acute financial constraints, the church could not afford to engage a composite construction contractor as the contractor's charge at least 20-25% of the project cost as their own consideration. The quality of work by such contractors also was in question. In the photograph are Mrs Kalyan Masih, Rev Col L. Massey and Vice Admiral Johnson standing in front of the temporary building of the church. (photo)

The financial requirements were put up to the Pastorate Committee with a request to permit Col. Parvez Shah, and team to execute the construction without further delay.

Though the Church was in no position to raise the full amount of Rs. 15 lakhs required for the completion of the construction work within the extended time frame, the construction had to

 1988 – 2004

begin as any further delay could have resulted in the cancellation of the allotment of the land. The Pastorate Committee permitted to start the construction work and the congregation started making their individual contributions and collecting donations for this Project. The construction work for the House of our Lord started in full swing in April 1997. A request was made to the Diocese of Delhi, CNI, for urgent financial help, but at that point in time, they could not extend any financial help as they were also facing financial problems.

It was recommended to the Pastorate Committee that the composite contractors will not be engaged for any of the works and only labour contractors will be hired for the project. Col. Parvez Shah took the responsibility to coordinate, oversee and organize the complete requirement of supervision of work, provisioning of construction materials, ensuring of quality control and speedy execution of the project.

The Pastorate Committee approved the proposal and; the labour contractor, Mr. Irshad from Bareilly, was hired. He had worked with Mr. Vaghela and was found to be very good, reliable and economical. He had his own team of masons, technicians, bar benders, operators and other support personnel required with him. They were good and reliable workers. This labour contract meant the Church team had to procure and provide all building materials including steel, bricks, cement, aggregate, (broken stones for making concrete) sand and everything else. They also had to do the accurate accounting for materials and ensure quality control for every item bought.-

On the same lines, but on item rate contract, the carpenter, Mr. Philip from Delhi was engaged, and all the carpentry/timber work, including the making of pews for the Church, was done by him. This also meant that all the provisioning, accounting and quality control, and supervision had to be done by Col. Parvez Shah, and his team. Similarly, the electricians, painters, hardware workers and all other workers were supervised, controlled and coordinated by him.

The work started in full swing and good speed, but now another serious challenge came up. The funds flow did not match the speed and progress of work which resulted in most of the purchases to be made on credit. It was very difficult and had to be managed and coordinated with requests and liaison with the suppliers, our fund providers and teams of workers. With God's grace, all suppliers were helpful, and we did not face any serious holdups and supply crises. So much so that the only purchases made on down payment by account payee cheques were for Teak Wood which was bought from wholesale timber market, Kirti Nagar, New Delhi, and electric materials, lights and fitments bought from the wholesale market, Chandni Chowk, Delhi.

The requirement of these stores was worked out to the exact quantities, converted into wholesale units and procured by the Purchase Committee, consisting of Col. Parvez Shah, Mr. Alex John, Mr. Ajit Massey, Mr. Patrick and Wg.Cdr. Ransford Cowasjee. Materials had to be sourced, bought and transported to Noida. This process though very laborious and tedious saved a considerable amount of money and good quality teak wood could be purchased for all the woodworks. In the same way, a lot of money could be saved for electrical fittings and materials of good quality could be purchased.

Thereafter the staircase was also constructed. The congregation kept up with generous donations towards the manufacture of all but five pews. Most of these pews carry the names of the donors on it. The marble top altar and pulpit were made using the marble arranged by late Mr. K.B. Lal. A beautiful teak wood Cross was placed on top of the Altar on the wall, which was donated by Wg Cdr. Ransford Cowasjee. The PA system was selected, procured and installed by Col. Lukose, with the help of the Sound Engineer of the Sound System Export Company. All other essentials were donated by the members of the congregation. Now with the grace of God and the generous help of congregation and able guidance of Presbyter-In-charge, Pastorate Committee, the most outstanding help and efforts of the fund-raising organization of the church, the complete and beautiful Christ Church came up. We are proud of it and thankful to our God Almighty.

The construction team had to work very hard and with the full and whole-hearted financial support, moral support and prayers of the congregation in December 1997 the main worship hall, boundary wall with the gate, interiors and almost 60% of our pews were ready and the Church edifice was consecrated to the glory of God on 7th December 1997 by the then Bishop of the Diocese of Delhi, Rt. Rev. Karam Masih. The joy and happiness of all those who contributed to this cause was beyond words. Praise to the Lord God Jesus Christ for his mercies.

The then Leader of the opposition of Lok Sabha, Shri Atal Bihari Vajpayee, (who later became the Prime Minister of India) congratulated the efforts of the Christian Congregation of Noida, especially that of Rev. Col. Lawrence Massey, the Pastorate Committee, Building Committee and the Congregation as a whole, for their coordination, volunteer efforts and leadership. He wrote to Rev. Col. Lawrence Massey, "I am aware this would not have taken place without the tireless efforts for Fund Raising by the entire congregation and without the coordination and leadership of yourself and the voluntary efforts of your pastoral and building committees…There are many lessons that can be learnt from this when people unite for a common cause and work with faith, anything is possible."

On a request, Immanuel Marthoma Church was given permission to worship twice a month, in our church till they constructed their own church building.

Services in Different Languages

The main worship service was then bi-lingual, in English and Hindi. On bifurcation, the first Hindi service was inaugurated and blessed by Rt. Rev. Pritam B. Santram, on 12 January 1992. Late Cdr. Neville Mullerworth (Retd) and late Mr. Kunj B. Lal, then DGM, DTC assisted Rev. Col. Lawrence Massey, in English and Evening Hindi service respectively. The evening service was later discontinued for a few genuine reasons.

It may be of interest to the readers that, much later, Rev. Dr. Paul Swarup combined the Hindi and English services into a bi-lingual service which was continued for several years even into the time of Rev. Kamal Mall, who succeeded him. However, again after detailed deliberations by the PC and AGM, separate services in Hindi (at 8 a.m.) and in English (at 9:45 a.m.) and combined bi-lingual service on 4th Sundays and on all Christian festivals was introduced.

On months with 5 Sundays, the services are led by, Sunday School children, Youth Fellowship, Women's Fellowship and Senior Member Fellowship on rotation.

Evening Praise and Worship Service, introduced by Rev. Dr Paul Swarup, continues to be held as bi-lingual services and has become very popular with Christians and people from other communities.

Contribution of the elders in the ministry of CCN

Rev. Col. Lawrence Massey was assisted by the organist Lt. Col. Victor Duraisami, (who passed away in Bangalore, a few years back), and was supported by Lt. Gen. E G. Kerr, in conducting the morning services. Sunday School for children was led by Mrs. Shunila Santram and a Prayer Group was led by Mrs. Pramila Lal. Mrs. Manorama Lukose joined this ministry in 1990.

As someone who has been associated with the church for decades, it would be appropriate to state here that Mrs. Manorama Lukose continued to serve the Lord in various manners for many years. Every Saturday she helped prepare the church for the Sunday worship. She often donated flowers for the Altar till other volunteers took over. People celebrating birthdays and anniversaries were encouraged to donate flowers for the altar also. Guided by Rev. Dr. Paul Swarup, she would prepare (also donated) the Altar linen in different colours and ensured that the caretakers are trained in preparing the Altar for each occasion and festival. Like many other members, she has liberally donated money and materials for the church Altar.

Maintenance of the Church and its Premises

In the initial years, CCN had meagre financial resources and could not outsource the maintenance and upkeep of the church. However, the sincere, and devoted members managed the maintenance of the church on their own. Wg. Cdr. Dennis Harrison mobilized the youth: Lukose boys, Dyes boys, Harrison girls, Alex's little fellow, and Cowasjee boys to keep the plot free of grass and to clean up the church premises, as remembered by Mrs. Helen Harrison. (She is one of our founding members, Ex-Secretary of the Pastorate Committee and former Principal of Somerville School, Greater Noida, who, on her retirement has joined Epiphany

Church, Gurgaon). The member families, on rotation, cleaned up the Chapel for Sunday worship services and took tremendous pride in keeping the Temple of God clean and tidy. Col. Lukose, then a PC member, with his family planted Asoka droplets trees alongside the drain and created a garden and maintained it for about three years.

Church Caretakers and Security

Since the days of the extended temporary church, CCN engaged caretakers for security and general upkeep of the church. The past and present caretakers were Mr. Goodwin, Mr. Didar Massey, Mr. Aman, Mr. Daniel, Mr. Rajan from Orissa, Mr. Robin, Mr. Daniel and now Mr. George Kattamala.

Mr. Ramesh Thapa has been the main security person since the time of Rev. Dr. Paul Swarup. Later, Rev. Kamal Mall included Mr. Ashok as the second security person as per a PC decision.Mr Ramkhilawan has been the church part-time gardner for decades.

Mr. Mohit, who joined the in 2013 is responsible for general upkeep and maintenance of the church.

Garden Fete

First Annual Garden Fete of CCN was held on the 13th November 1997 in a combined celebration of anniversary and to raise funds for paying for Church construction bills and later in 1998 and 1999 for making payment towards sundry expenditures. Rt. Rev. Karam Masih, then Bishop of Diocese of Delhi, CNI, inaugurated the fete while Rev. Paul Swarup, then Secretary of the Diocese of Delhi, accompanied him and was present for the inaugural/ dedication service as well. Subsequently, Rev. Dr. Paul Swarup, made it a regular feature and Church Fete is now held, every year from 2004. These events greatly enabled the church to raise funds for the subsequent construction work, and later for supporting the outreach activities of the Church.

Noida Christian Welfare Association (NCWA)

It was in those days, NCWA, a Registered Body, comprising 5 mainline churches of Noida: namely, Christ Church-CNI, St Mary's Roman Catholic Church, Orthodox Syrian Church, Immanuel Mar Thoma Church and the Bethel Methodist Church, took birth, with Rev. Col. Lawrence Massey and Mr. Rohit David from CCN elected to its Governing Body. This idea was mooted way back on the 12thOctober 1989, by all denominations of that period, under the Secretary-ship of Rev. John Joseph, Evangelical Church. The newly formed NCWA held its 1st Governing Body Meeting on 21st January 2001. Its aim was the promotion of Christian unity and welfare and for organised representation for the allotment of land for a Christian Cemetery in Noida.

A name that needs special mention here is that of Dr. Mathews, whose contact with the Principal Secretary of Uttar Pradesh, paved the way for the allotment of the land for a Christian cemetery in Noida.

President of NCWA was to be a priest, on rotation amongst the five mainline churches, and the Secretary from a church other than that of the President. It is noteworthy that the first Secretary of NCWA, Mr. Rohit David, belonged to CCN. He gave a definite shape to NCWA. After a year of devoted service, Mr. Rohit David handed over the charge to Col. M. L. Lukose, CCN, who held the post from the time of the Registration of the NCWA on 27 May 2003 till the allotment of the Cemetery in June 2008, and its dedication on Sunday, 29th June 2008. All the systems were put in place and the Constitution for the Cemetery was approved in the First Annual General Body Meeting of NCWA and distributed to all by Col. Lukose.

He handed over the charge of Secretary-ship to Dr. Helen Sekar, and subsequently Mr. Anandkumar Peter, both from CCN, also pitched in their support to the NCWA as its General Secretary. And now Mr.Abraham Daniel, CCN, a person with much association with other churches has been elected as the General Secretary of NCWA. Wg. Cdr. Reginald Mukha (Retd), Wg. Cdr. Ransford Cowasjee and his wife Mrs. Kamna Cowasjee are other names of CCN that should find mention here, as they diligently attended all the meetings of NCWA for all these years. Similarly, Dr. Mathews and the Meshy family, remained in the forefront of the Christmas Float and Procession. Our church continues to contribute as Presidents, and members of the Governing Body and Cemetery Committee, as per its Constitution and with financial support as needed.

The first burial in the newly acquired Christian Cemetery was held on the 4th March 2009 of Mrs. Rosy M Moukam, with the burial conducted by Fr. John F. D'Cunha of St. Mary's Church.

Superannuation of Rev. Col. Lawrence Massey

During the 17 eventful years, Rev. Col. Lawrence Massey worked as an honorary Priest. Often repeated Bible quote of Rev. Col. Lawrence Massey was from John 15:4-5, "Abide in me, and I in you. As the branch cannot bear the fruit of itself, unless it abides in the vine, neither can you, unless you abide in me. "I am the vine; you are the branches. He who abides in me, and I in him, bears much fruit; for without me you can do nothing." He understood the inner meaning of the passage so well and had delivered a series of sermons based on this theme. We recollect that during those days when CCN did not have an organist, Rev. Col. Lawrence Massey preferred the congregation to sing as opening hymns, the evergreen hymns 'Holy, Holy, Holy, Lord God Almighty". 'Blessed Assurance', 'There shall be showers of blessing' and 'What a friend we have in Jesus' were some other favourites.

On superannuation, Rev. Col. Lawrence Massey handed over the charge of the church to Rev. Dr. Paul Swarup in April 2004. By then the membership of the Church, from the initial 13 had grown to about 125 families with over 300 worshipers. On festival days people used to attend in troves and tents were needed to be erected for them.

Our Bishop and Pastors

Rt. Rev. Warris K. Masih

Rev. Col. L. Massey

Rev. Dr. Paul Swarup

Rev. Kamal Mall

Rev. Sunil S. Ghazan

Rev. Bani

Rev. Varun Alfred

Rev. Sachin

Rev. Lomesh

CHRISTMAS

Church Annual Fete and Ekta Utsav

Defence Sunday

Senior Members Fellowship Sunday

Adivasi Sunday

Church Outreach Programmes

Non-formal Education and Schooling of Children

Entrepreneur Development Project - Tailoring Program

Bible Study

60 Minutes in the Chair

Lent Sunday Group

Vacation Bible School Ministry

Other Functions

Deaf Fellowship

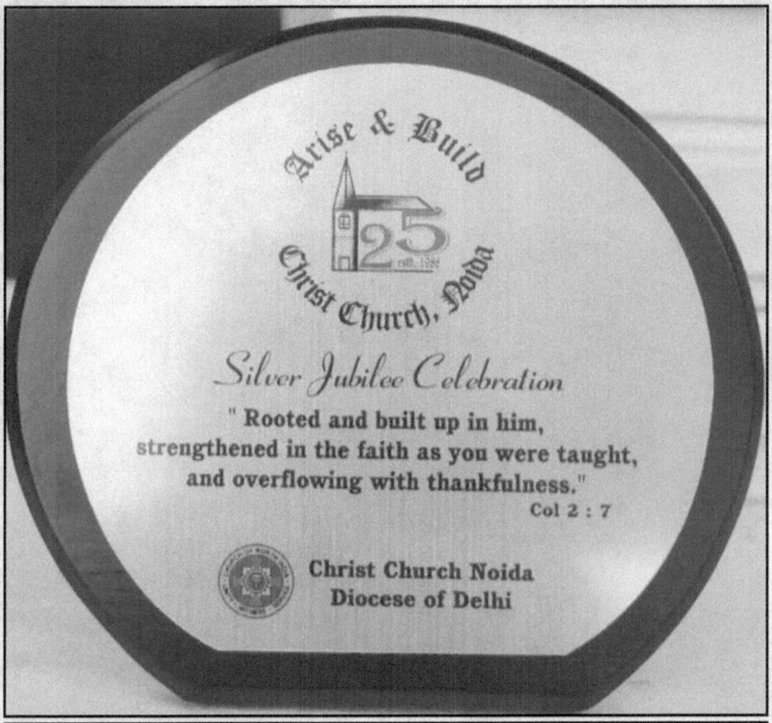

Arise & Build

25 estd. 1984

Christ Church, Noida

Silver Jubilee Celebration

" Rooted and built up in him,
strengthened in the faith as you were taught,
and overflowing with thankfulness."

Col 2 : 7

**Christ Church Noida
Diocese of Delhi**

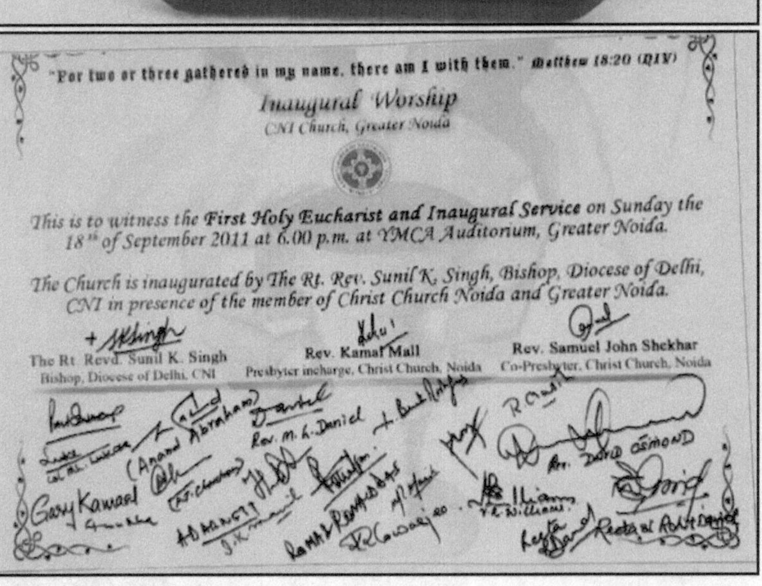

First Church Building

New Shepherd

Distribution of blankets

Choir

2004 — 2011

An Era of Spiritual Revitalisation

The dynamic leadership of Rev. Dr. Paul Swarup re-energised the life and ministry of CCN during the period from 2004 to 2011. Rev. Dr Paul Swarup is a scholar having obtained PhD in Old Testament Theology/Dead Sea Scrolls, University of Cambridge, UK – Faculty of Oriental Studies; Advanced level Biblical Hebrew from Hebrew University of Jerusalem Summer School; Th.M. Old Testament & Semitics from Princeton Theological Seminary, USA; M.Th. Old Testament from United Theological College, Bangalore; BD from Union Biblical Seminary, Pune; B.A- English Literature from Madras Christian College, Chennai. He is a linguist and a good administrator. He carefully chose the people who would help him in his ministry at CCN. He has the unique distinction of being the only Priest of South East Asia, to be selected for Translation and Revision of the NIV Bible. He is also a member of the Editors Group of South Asia Bible Commentary.

Rev. Dr. Paul Swarup ushered in an era of refinements, improvements and order and system in all aspects of church life. He functioned strictly within the framework of the CNI

Constitution and the law of the land. He set for himself and declared his Episcopal vision and never deviated from it. Divine services witnessed spiritual upliftment. He did not tolerate any aberration in the theological ethics. It was during this period Rev. Dr. Paul Swarup recommended to the Bishop of the Diocese of Delhi and installed 5 lay leaders, namely Vice Admiral H. Johnson, Anandkumar Peter, Col. M. L. Lukose, Brig. Rajiv Williams, and Mr. Rohit David, thus encouraging the laity to conduct services and preach meaningful messages. He also inducted elders of good standing to the Pastorate Committee, after obtaining due sanction from the Bishop of Delhi.

The Formal Roster of Church Members

Rev. Dr. Paul Swarup prepared the first Members Roster, after taking over as the Presbyter-in-charge. Names of worshipers, who till then had submitted applications for membership of the Church were included. It was computerised and as of 5th February 2006, it recorded a total of 388 members including children of 123 families; featuring 312 Communicant members. (Incidentally, when he handed over charge to Rev. Kamal Mall, after serving CCN for 7 years, the church had about 215 families and over 600 individual members on the roles.) The fact remains that not all filed applications to become members, and many just continued to worship without putting in any written application for membership. Some of these faithful regularised their membership subsequently. At the same time, some of the faithful who did not file an application but whose names featured in some early documents were listed as having joined the church as on 13 November 1988.

Rev. Dr. Paul Swarup handed over this task of preparing and updating of the Church roster to Mr. Stalin, a young enthusiastic engineer who put in much time in the service of the church, and Mr Anandkumar Peter, who is computer savvy, to expand on the details of members, and to create an identification number system for families and members. This was done going back to the file maintained of membership applications by Rev. Dr. Paul Swarup, carefully filed in chronological order. It is cautioned here that this record also suffers from the same deficiency as those who were worshipping regularly in the church but did not submit a membership application may not have been recorded. This computerised record is being regularly updated, in the order of approval of membership applications by the Pastorate Committee, by Mrs. Christy Franklin, the Church Administrator.

Spiritual initiatives from 2004 - 2011

Bible Study Groups during Lent

Rev. Dr. Paul Swarup introduced Study groups of our congregants residing in various sectors of Noida, Mayur Vihar and Ghaziabad. He took pains to prepare study materials and questions for the groups to use well in advance, based on the topic decided for the year. He would select suitable people to lead each group and train them to handle the Bible study in their respective groups. This has become a regular feature in CCN, and participants look forward to these study sessions. Mr. Peter, Mr. Earnest Clark, now Dr. Earnest Clark (then an American missionary in India) and Mr. Babu assisted Rev. Dr. Paul Swarup, in preparation of study notes, for Lenten Study. Church Administrator, Mrs. Christy Franklin, managed the printing and distribution of the study materials and scheduling of venues for each week. The study material prepared on the theme 'The Holy Spirit' was later published as a book by Rev. Dr. Paul Swarup

Annual Spiritual Retreats for members

Another valuable programme for the spiritual upliftment of members in the form of an Annual Spiritual Retreat was started by Rev. Dr. Paul Swarup. Voluntary participants, numbering about 50 were transported to out-station location, (initially at the Himalayan Torch Bearers, on the way to Missouri) and three days of in-depth discourse and discussions were held. Besides Rev. Dr. Paul Swarup, Bishop Santram, Mr. Peter and co-presbyters and deacons in service were regular resource people. Participants returned spiritually refreshed from these retreats.

Vacation Bible School

The first VBS (Vacation Bible School) in CCN was conducted from 8th to 14th June 2009, under the initiative of the then Hon. Treasurer Mr. Anandkumar Peter, as its Director, ably assisted by Mrs. Christy Franklin, Mr. Shibu George, and Mrs. Aruna Romulus for administrative functions and dedicated teachers including, Mrs. Valentina Muthumani, Mrs. Ruth Nath, Mrs. Manorama Lukose, Mrs. Vineeta Williams, Ms. Margret Meshy, to name a few, with the guidance and monitoring by the Parish Priest, Rev. Dr. Paul Swarup. Mrs Christy Franklin continues to render help for VBS year after year. Children of the church and those from churches and of other denominations and even from other faiths attend the Vacation Bible School and it is a grand success. It has now become an annual event with an ever-increasing number of participants, touching 175 or more. Praise to the Lord for blessing this ministry. Mr. Peter remains committed to this ministry and teaches senior students every year and holds devotion sessions for the teachers and volunteers.

The team from Trans-Yamuna Youth for Christ, in conjunction with members of CCN Youth were an immense blessing to VBS Praise and Worship segment which was supported and encouraged by then Presbyter-in-charge, Revd. Kamal Mall. He promoted the Trans-Yamuna Youth for Christ ministry and during this period the Director of Trans-Yamuna Youth for Christ was made Director of VBS for few consecutive years. VBS grew in popularity with the help of teachers, volunteers, mostly from members of Youth of CCN and the Sunday School.

Wednesday Prayer Cell

Prayer meeting every Wednesday evening was introduced. Rev. Dr. Paul Swarup and his wife Mrs. Nina Swarup made it a point to attend the prayer cell on a regular basis. People with illnesses from all faiths attended the prayer cell and special prayers by laying of hands was performed. His prayer had helped those in sickness and in distress. Some of the families of other faiths who experienced the blessings and obtained peace joined our Church. Wednesday meet continues till date. Mrs. Manorama Lukose has been assisting the pastors for many years. Later Ms. Stella Miller, Mrs. Leila Varki, Mrs. Rita Gill, Mrs. Roma Das and Mr. Ronny Das and deacons and priests associated with Christ Church have taken the lead in these Wednesday prayers.

Evening Praise and Worship Service and Choir

An evening Praise and Worship service was introduced in 2008 by Rev. Dr. Paul Swarup. Mr. Peter assisted him in the conduct of the service. Books of the Bible were selected and studied on Sunday evenings. The Service would begin with praise and worship, followed by Bible. The Book of Jeremiah was the first to be taken up by Rev. Dr. Paul Swarup followed by Paul's Epistle to the

Ephesians by Mr. Peter. This continued till Rev. Bani joined as an Associate Presbyter and assisted in the worship.

The choir received a boost when Mr. Martin, an accomplished organist became a member of the church. He supported the evening worship service regularly. Mr. Ronald Das also joined the in the evening and was entrusted with the task of deciding suitable Praise & Worship songs for Sunday. Mr. Das who is a good singer and a guitarist, later joined by his wife Mrs. Roma Naomi Das, began to lead the Service. The couple continues to conduct the evening service in CCN. Ms. Stella Miller, Mr. Joseph Immanuel, Mrs. Preeti Joseph, Dr. Leila Varkey and Mr. Alex John, present youth leader, take great interest in conducting the Praise & Worship service on rotation. Col. Lukose also took an active role in the evening service, occasionally.

The visual presentation of the message was introduced during this service when the first projector was received as a gift from an anonymous source which was replaced by a new projector contributed by Dr. Mrs. Helen Sekar. Mr. Peter assisted in the preparation of PowerPoint slides. And later, these days this is being done by Mrs. Roma Naomi Das.

Expository Bible Study

One day workshop was conducted for all those who were interested in the Expository Methods of Bible study. During the workshop, the participants were encouraged to preach on the passage they studied. All the interested participants were given an opportunity to preach during the evening Service. Book of Romans was included in the Study.

Church planting at Greater Noida

Recognising the fact that Greater Noida was without a CNI church, Rev. Dr. Paul Swarup planted the seed to start a worship service in the premises of YMCA, Greater Noida in the year 2009-2010. This was started as an extension of CCN. Services were conducted by Rev. Samuel John Sekar and Rev. Bani. Mr. P.J. Chauhan, who had taken up residence in Greater Noida and a member of YMCA facilitated this effort. He inspired CCN members resident in Greater Noida, to regularly attend the Sunday Service at Greater Noida and to arrange and prepare the YMCA hall for the worship. Subsequently, he organised retreats and seminars, picnics there. On 18th September 2011, the then Parish Priest, Rev. Kamal Mall arranged the formal dedication cum Inaugural Divine Eucharist Service presided over by Rt. Rev. Sunil K. Singh, the then Bishop of Diocese of Delhi, CNI, at the YMCA auditorium, Greater Noida, thus formalising the existence of Greater Noida Christ Church extension.

Short Workshops and Spiritual Discourses

On National holidays such as Independence Day and Republic Day, short-half day spiritual workshops and spiritual discourses were conducted after hoisting the National Flag and singing of the National Anthem. Members attended these workshops in good number.

Training by the Haggai Institute in Evangelism

Initially, some of our members were sponsored by the church to attend a 3 days' workshop conducted at the Methodist Church in Lodhi Road. Later, as a measure to help larger participation, CCN, as initiated by Mr. Peter invited the Haggai Institute to conduct a workshop in our parish hall. A second workshop at

CCN especially for the Hindi congregation was organised by Mr. Rohit David. Several members benefited and were awarded certificates of participation by the Haggai Institute.

Ordinates and Associate Pastors

Rev. Samuel John Sekar after a year of service at CCGN was transferred to St. Stephen Chapel, Delhi. Mr.Derik Daman Rogers was trained for 6 months under Rev. Dr. Paul Swarup. He was ordained as Deacon and was transferred to Ambala. Soon in the year 2008, Rev. Bani joined CCN as the co- presbyter. After Rev. Bani was transferred to Kalka, Dn. Varun Alfred and subsequently Dn. Sachin were trained in our Church and after a year of service at Greater Noida and Noida, they were ordained and transferred as priests to various churches under CNI. Rev. Lomesh Chand, a missionary, was posted as a co- presbyter to CCN in 2017 and worked as Presbyter –in- Charge of CCGN. He did a lot of missionary work in and around Greater Noida, Noida and adjacent areas before he was transferred to Ashirwad Church, Mayur Vihar in April 2018

CCN Outreach Efforts

As the church grew internally, Rev. Dr. Paul Swarup decided to look outward to engage with the society through various outreach programmes.

Non-formal Education for Unschooled Children

Then a member of the Pastorate Committee, Dr. Mrs. Helen Sekar, (Ministry of Labour, Govt of India) as part of her assignment in her organisation had conducted a survey in various pockets in and around Noida, on children engaged in rag-picking. The survey revealed that nearly 1000 children of migrant workers were forced into this work and were never offered an opportunity to attend a school like other children. CCN decided that such children along with other children in localities of Noida would be the best target to impart non-formal education. Thus, in 2007 Rev. Dr. Paul Swarup identified the neighbouring slum 'Chalera' for the outreach work and the Outreach Programme known as Chalera Project was initiated.

Programme coordination was entrusted to Mrs. Kamna Cowasjee who identified about 70 children for this purpose and shouldered all the responsibilities efficiently, overseen by Rev. Dr. Paul Swarup and Mr. Anand Peter. Dr. Helen Sekar offered her support to the programme for several years. The seed funding for the project which helped us to start the project came from the Mustard Seed Foundation, USA, for three years, sourced by Mr. Peter.

Initially, the programme was conducted for half a day in the Chalera Village Chowpal. In 2008, some of these children were upgraded and the segregated into groups who attained Class 1 Standard/ Proficiency and were moved to our church complex, utilizing funds donated by M/S Jindals, through Brig. Williams. (Incidentally, Brig. Williams is the present Director of Outreach programmes and runs it assisted by Mrs. Christy Franklin.) On attaining proficiency of Class 3 / 4 grade, some of these children were admitted to nearby Public Schools, with some of our church members sponsoring and providing full financial and counselling support. All children were provided with uniforms, books and refreshments.

Subsequently, its plans and programmes, having been revised, and all children were moved to Church building complex. The Church has been generating and spending approx. Rs 9-10 lakhs each year for this outreach project, by way of salary for teachers, stationery, conveyance and aids for Children, rent for the premises etc.

From 2016 onwards, elementary education is provided to these children steered by Mrs. Poonam Runda and efforts are being made to get them admitted preferably in government schools.

Women's Empowerment through Vocational Training

In 2009 a Tailoring Training Unit was established for the women of nearby Harijan Basti. On completion of successful training Merit Certificates were issued to them by M/S Usha International, the Sewing Machine Company. Now the Tailoring and Empowering Unit has also been moved to the Church Building Complex.

Alcoholic Anonymous Meeting Facility

In 2009, CCN decided to allow the Alcoholic Anonymous Group to conduct meetings with a view to de-addict them from Alcoholism, once a week at the Sunday School Room of the multi utility facility. Spiritual inputs were imparted by Rev. Dr. Paul Swarup, to the participants and as a social gesture, refreshments were provided by the Church during their meetings.

Theological Education Support

Committed to furthering Theological education, Rev. Dr. Paul Swarup initiated the creation of a fund for this purpose. Besides the contributions by church members, it was decided that all 'Denial Contribution during Lent' be dedicated for this purpose. Since then CCN has been supporting financially 3 to 4 Theological Trainee Pastors at Bishop's College Kolkata and Union Biblical Seminary, Pune, recognised in imparting theological education and training of priests and award of Degrees. Rev. Bani, one of our priests, has also been granted financial assistance to pursue B.D. programme at Bishop's College, Kolkata.

Hearing Impaired Fellowship

Another blessing of God, during the tenure of Rev. Dr. Paul Swarup, was the establishment of a Deaf Fellowship in our Church, under the leadership of Mr. Zorin Daud Singha and his family in June 2008. Their children, especially, Angel, Asha and Michael Singha translated the service for them in sign language. New members of this group were baptized, confirmed and made members of the Church. Sign language translation of the Divine Services has become a regular feature at CCN Services. This Fellowship, under the guidance of the Rev. Kamal Mall, has grown to over 75 strong. They are proud to be members of our Church.

Financial Management and Control

Rev. Dr. Paul Swarup chose Anandkumar Peter, a Chartered Management Accountant by profession, a new member of the PC, to assist the then Hon. Treasurer, Col. M. L. Lukose in streamlining the accounts, finance and enforce internal checks and control in the financial management of the Church during 2005. Mr. Peter took over from Col. M. L. Lukose as the Hon. Treasurer after Col. Lukose completed his tenure and has been the Hon. Treasurer for several years in two stints. He continues to oversee the accounts, quarterly reporting, and annual audits, besides the preparation of annual budgets.

The ensuing period saw a tremendous increase in the revenues of the church with member contributions and donations, both in-house and external sources showing manifold growth. This, in turn, helped CCN to invest in capital projects and various other projects initiated by Rev. Dr. Paul Swarup.

Audit of the church accounts by an external auditor, Mr. George Koshi of M/s Koshi and Koshi was done for the first time for the financial year 2005-2006 during the treasurership of Col. Lukose, assisted by Mr. Peter in line with the financial prudence policy of Rev. Dr. Paul Swarup. Mr. George Koshi has been auditing our account voluntarily for years.

Construction of Multi-utility Building and Parish Hall

Rev. Dr. Paul Swarup went into an accelerated drive to generate funds for the building projects. Conducting Annual Garden Fete was revived, first during his time in November 2004, right from the very first year of his joining the CCN and thereafter every year in November or December. It is notable that barring a contribution of Rupee 1 lakh by the Diocese of Delhi, CCN generated funds for both the building projects, Parsonage-cum-multi utility facility and the Parish Hall, totalling to over Rs. 65 lakhs.

Multi-utility Building

After the Parsonage cum Multi- Utility Complex was built, Rev. Dr. Paul Swarup, till then living in a rented flat moved into this parsonage with his wife Nina and son Daniel. They were the first occupants of this parsonage. This complex also accommodated a hall for Sunday School and residence for a Caretaker. The washrooms for the congregants attending the Church are situated in this building. The foundation stone of the parsonage was laid on the 27 March 2005 by Bishop Karam Masih, then Bishop of the Diocese of Delhi, CNI and the building was dedicated to the glory of God, also by him on the 8th of January 2006.

Parish Hall and the Steeple Complex

The Multi-Purpose Parish Hall, on the first floor of the Church building, was then constructed during the time of Rev. Dr. Paul Swarup. Its Foundation Stone was laid on the 22nd April 2007 by Bishop Karam Masih and consecrated on its completion on 30th March 2008 by the then Bishop, Rt. Rev. Sunil Singh. The vertical extension to the main church building consisted of a large parish hall with a stage, a tall steeple containing the specially fabricated Church bell, a storeroom and a pantry on either side of the stage, and similar two rooms on the in-between floor. One of the rooms is assigned as a guest room for the visiting clergy, and the other as a workroom for the Presbyter-in-charge. Presently, the Presbyter's office is being used by the Tailoring unit. A separate bath and toilet were also constructed under the staircase for the use of the visiting clergy.

Church Bell

A brass bell was donated by Brig. Rajiv Williams and family which was functional in the Church until the new steeple was built. Need for a larger bell arose. Dr. Matthew, then a regular contributing member of the church organized and financed the fabrication of the Church bell which was installed at the top of the steeple. The Church complex had a new look befitting its vantage location. He had been beautifully decorating the Church on festivals with fresh flowers, till he changed residence to New Delhi. On installation of the new bell, the old bell was donated to a church in Sattal, with the consent of Brig. Williams, through the good office of Rev. Murch.

Baptismal Font

For purposes of adult baptism CCN constructed a Baptismal pond at the rear of the Church. Till then CCN did not have a Baptismal pond. Adult candidates for baptism had to go to Turkman Gate church for baptism. This was remedied by creating a marble laid

Baptismal pond /font on the side of the church building. For child baptism a portable font is available in the Church.

All these were made possible through the dedicated co-operation and participation of the parishioners ably guided and inspired by Rev. Dr. Paul Swarup. CCN felt a new spiritual vigour and its congregation continued to be highly motivated.

Diesel Generator

A 24 KVA generator was installed in the Complex to ensure uninterrupted power supply during worship and other functions, a laudable effort by the then PC members, especially Mr. Victor Franklin, Mr. Shibu George and Mr. Rohit David, with the support of the Treasurer Mr. Peter who organised the funding.

Church Website

The church website, www.christchurchnoida.org, was launched with the help of Mr. Anandkumar Peter, who continues to update and maintain it for CCN. Rev. Dr. Paul Swarup encouraged and motivated him and personally worked with him on the contents of the website and guided him on the design and layout of the same.

Weekly Flyer

A well designed and informative flyer was introduced during this period for each weekly Divine Service and for special occasions. It also listed the names of people who were sick or in distress and needed prayer support from the parishioners apart from birthday and anniversary greetings, appreciation and regular notices on upcoming events of the Church and the Diocese.

Fellowships and Sunday School

Much attention was paid for the progress of Women's Fellowship, Youth Fellowship and the Sunday School. To encourage these Christian spiritual and service activities, fifth Sundays of the month were dedicated to them. The Fellowship members conducted the morning service and delivered the message. The Fellowship members participated in all church activities, especially in the Annual Fete, apart from their respective meetings and activities.

Church Choir

CCN Choir received shot in the arm when Mr Martin a highly talented organist joined the church, after the departure of Col. Victor Duraisami. Mr. Martin, besides attending the morning Service would diligently attend the evening Praise & Worship Service. He would join the carol singers with his accordion. When he visited Canada on an official trip from his office, appreciating his talent at the local church there, and the contributions he is making in the Indian Church, CCN, the Canadians donated a Church Organ for the use of CCN. It was shipped to India at their cost and was in use at the church for several years.

After Mr. Martin was transferred out of Noida, Mr. Richard Muthumani, though not an organist, assumed the role of the Choir Director. He was assisted by his wife Mrs. Valentina Muthumani and used a talented young schoolboy Wilson as the organist. Choir organisation became formal at this stage. Mr. Ravindran Sunder Singh, an organist joined the Choir and later took over as Choir Master and continues to be the Choir Master of CCN, till now. Choir conducted Canticles and special programmes during Christmas season and other occasions.

2011 — 2018

Rev. Dr. Paul Swarup, after an illustrious, satisfying and fruitful stint of 7 years, and having sown the seed for the Greater Noida Congregation, handed over charge of the church to the incoming Presbyter-in-charge Rev. Kamal Mall, in April 2011. Rev. Kamal Mall gave further impetus to all the activities established by Rev. Dr. Paul Swarup. His motto being, "Be exalted, O God, above the heavens, And Your glory above all the earth;" - Psalms. 108: 5.

Rev. Kamal Mall pastored the church to greater heights. He believed in greater participation of the younger generation and the women of the Church, in all the ministries. Though he did not formally renew the licenses of lay leaders, who were earlier installed, he continued to utilise their services. After bringing in few people as Bishops nominees to the Pastorate Committee in the initial years, he decided not to recommend names to the Bishop for the nomination in the later years. He inducted more young people and women in the Pastorate Committee and involved them in all the activities of the Church.

During his second year as the Presbyter-in-Charge of CCN, Rev. Kamal Mall was elected as the Treasurer of Diocese of Delhi,

CNI, first for a period of 3 years and then for a further period of another 3 years. The congregation was so proud that their priest has been so elected, faced the absence of the Priest from the Parish with patience. It was indeed a challenge for him to manage the dual portfolio, but he tried to balance it as much as he could. However, the joining of Rev. Lomesh Chand, with good evangelical traits, as co- presbyter, though at the fag-end of his tenure at CCN, filled up whatever vacuum was felt by the congregation, both at CCN and at Greater Noida. It goes to Rev. Kamal Mall's credit that he pursued the efforts of his predecessor Rev. Dr. Paul Swarup and took the spiritual activities of both the congregation.

Silver Jubilee Celebrations

CCN celebrated its Silver Jubilee in the year 2013 with the motto 'Arise and Build". Celebrations were planned and initiated with great gusto and conducted through a period of the whole of one-year 2013, under the able stewardship of Rev. Kamal Mall, and the enthusiastic co-operation of all parishioners. Rev. Kamal Mall proved his leadership abilities and organisational capabilities during the conduct of these events.

Medical Camp

Silver Jubilee celebrations started with a Medical Camp held at the church premises, on 28th April 2013, ably organized and overseen by Dr. Kanishk Williams, a member of our Church, equally and ably supported by Mr. Sachin Daniel. Women's Fellowship (WFCS) and the Youth Fellowship actively participated as volunteers supporting the Medical Team from St. Stephen's Hospital, Delhi. Doctors, including Dr. Mrs. Lucky Chandekar, Dr. Vinita Daniel and Dr. Deepti Cecil and paramedics who were members of the church, were at the forefront of the activities on that day.

More than 700 men, women and children were provided medical examination, advice and prescriptions by specialist doctors of St. Stephen's Hospital, Delhi, consisting of Cardiologists, Orthopaedics, Physiotherapists, Dentists, Dieticians, Gynaecologists, Oncologists and Paediatricians. Quick lab tests were conducted to detect blood sugar.

Main beneficiaries of the Camp were members of NCWA, our Church, villagers from nearby localities and even passers-by. In certain cases, medicines were also given. WFCS of the Church under the leadership of Mrs. Manorama Lukose, assisted by Mr. Jeremiah Jai Babu provided refreshments to all participants throughout the day.

The Camp was inaugurated by Shri Dr. Mahesh Sharma, local MLA and owner of Kailash Hospital, Noida. And the concluding ceremony was presided over by former Naval Chief of Staff Admiral Sushil Kumar, a member of our Church. His closing words were inspirational to the Medical Team and participants. He distributed mementoes and certificates to all members of the Medical team.

Tree Plantation

Tree plantation was organised on Easter Sunday of 2013 at the Church garden by the congregation, after the Divine Service. Bishops, priests, women and the congregation took an active part in planting trees in the Church compound. Three decorative trees were planted along the front boundary by Rev. Col. Lawrence Massey, Bishop Santram and Rev. Kamal Mall.

Maha-Sangati

Maha-Sangati, with a special motto, "Make a joyful noise to the Lord, all the lands; Serve the Lord with gladness; come into his presence with singing. Psalms 100:1-2., was organised and led by Mr. Sachin Abraham Daniel. Multiple activities were held on 15th August 2013, after the celebration of and the usual associated with it. Highlights of Maha Sangati were:

- Initial 'praise and worship' by the entire congregation of over 300;

- Competitive items by 4 Groups- "Marvelling Marks, Rocking Peters, Thundering Johns and Dashing Daniels;

- Fancy Dress by church children;

- Quick Bible Reading competition;

- Bible Quiz;

- Group Songs, wherein Bishop Santram and Pastor also took part;

- Skit by Deaf Fellowship

Maha Sangati culminated with a social lunch.

Sports Festival

A Sports festival was conducted, over a period of 2 months, under the leadership of Dn. Varun Alfred, in the CCN premises. Games and sports organised included: VolleyBall, Throw Ball, Badminton, Tug of War and in-doors games such as Chess, Sudoku, Carom, and Arm Wrestling. Teams carried the same group names as in Maha Sangati. It was a surprise to see the then 82-year-old Mr. Vinay Cecil, father of Dr. Deepti Cecil participating in the Badminton competition. Members ofthe Hearing Impaired Fellowship also participated in the games. Mr. Suhail Titus was the all-rounder Referee.

Women's Retreat

A Women's Retreat was conducted on 13th July 2013 at our church under the leadership of then President of WFCS, Mrs. Shannon Mukha. Chief Guests-cum-Resource persons were Mrs. Sherilyn and Mrs. Vineeta Shaw. The retreat started with a prayer by Rev. Kamal Mall and a devotional song by Mrs Neeta Mall, and daughters Michelle and Minhael. Speakers from our church were Mrs Manorama Lukose and Dr Mrs Helen Sekar. Members of 12 Churches and Institutions of Diocese of Delhi, CNI & NCR participated. The participants were recognised with prizes and mementoes given away by Mrs Lily Abraham (Late), former president of WFCS and Mrs. Kamna Cowasjee, convenor of Silver Jubilee Celebrations.

Men's Retreat

A Men' Retreat was conducted on Saturday the 14th September 2013 in our Church under the leadership of Mr. Luke Chandekar. Highlights being discourse by Rev. Mohit Hitter on, "Arise and Build: The Role of Christian Men in Building the Family and Society". Song Competition, Solo Song and Bible Quiz. Social Lunch of Chinese Cuisine format was also served to the participants of 12 churches of NCR.

Inter-Denominational Children Festival

An Inter-denominational Children Festival drawn from all the NCWA and other churches was also conducted in 2013, as part of the Silver Jubilee Celebrations, under the able stewardship of

Mrs Roma Naomi Das. 98 children participated in the Bible Quiz, Bible verse memory competition, Short skits on Biblical themes, Slogan writing etc. The team of Trans-Yamuna Youth for Christ engaged in Praise & Worship along with members of the youth of CCN which the children enjoyed to the maximum. Youth volunteers & elders and Priests of the NCWA Churches participated in the whole event. 33 Children of our Church and 40 of Immanuel Marthoma Church participated in it; the rest of the participants were children from other churches of NCWA. Children's Fest has now become an annual activity since then, taken up by NCWA.

Vacation Bible School

2013 Vacation Bible School was held under the banner of Christ Church Silver Jubilee Celebrations at Somerville School International. Children of other Churches and faiths apart from those of CCN attended in large number as usual.

Silver Jubilee Logo Competition

There was a 'Silver Jubilee Logo' competition amongst the Youth. Mr. William Massey & Mr. Philip Nath jointly won the competition their design having been approved and used for the Silver Jubilee events, especially for the Brochure Cover.

Silver Jubilee Souvenir

A Souvenir was brought out on this occasion of the Silver Jubilee with Mrs. Kamna Cowasjee as the Convener and Chief Editor supported by Mrs. Roma Das and others including Dn. Varun, Mr. Sachin Daniel, Dr. Kanishk Williams, Ms. Margret Meshy, Mr. Philip Nath, Mr. Vinay Ralph, Ms. Angel Singha, Ms. Stella

Miller and Dr. Mrs. Helen Sekar. The Silver Jubilee Logo created by the creative efforts of Mr. William Meshy & Mr. Philip Nath adorned the cover page of the Souvenir.

The Souvenir was a unique one with several articles bringing out the memories of 25 years of existence of CCN. The contributors of this book acknowledge with gratefulness, all those who sent in information used in this book. This souvenir was released by Bishop of Delhi Rt. Rev. Sunil K Singh during the evening service celebrations on 13 November 2013. All Bishops, present and past and Priests of Diocese of Delhi participated in the grand service held in the evening. Governor and Chief Minister of UP were also magnanimous in greeting and appreciating the good work and progress of CCN in 25 years.

Our newsletter 'The Scroll'

The first edition of our quarterly Newsletter, 'The Scroll' was rolled out on 13th November 2013. The Scroll was conceived and proposed by Mr. Anandkumar Peter and supported by Rev. Kamal Mall and approved in the AGM, thus fulfilling a long-cherished dream. Rev. Kamal Mall and Mr. Peter created an editorial team with Mr. Peter heading it as its Chief Editor. The First Edition dated 13th November 2013 was distributed to all the guests and members during the Silver Jubilee Finale. The Scroll continues to be published at regular intervals with the help of Resident Editors, Mr. John Solomon, Mrs. Lukose and Mrs. Kamna Cowasjee.

Grand Finale

The Celebrations culminated in a grand finale Divine Service lead by the Bishop of Diocese of Delhi, Rt. Rev. Sunil Singh and several members of the clergy, including the Founder Presbyter

Rev Col Massey and the second presbyter, Rev. Dr. Paul Swarup in attendance. Rev. Dr. Paul Swarup delivered the key message. Every activity saw the leadership and managerial capabilities of Rev. Kamal Mall.

Senior Member Fellowship (SMF)

Conceptualised by Mr. Peter and duly supported by Rev. Kamal Mall a proposal to form a Senior Member Fellowship of members of both genders above 60 years of age, was duly approved in the AGM. Mr. Abraham Daniel was nominated as its Convenor. The fellowship primarily visited many house-bound members of the church. Conducted a film show on St. Peter & St. Paul, hosted a short discourse on the Passion of Christ. At this writing, the Fellowship is being managed by Brig. Rajiv Williams and Mrs. Kamna Cowasjee as its Convenor and Co-convenor respectively. It has been streamlined with an annual quarterly programme to include visit to old-age homes as apart from ongoing home visits, celebrating of Defence Sunday and conjointly holding stalls in the annual fete.

60 Minutes in the Chair

As part of the efforts of SMF, a Bible Study programme was initiated by Mr. Peter known as 60 minutes in the Chair. Classes were conducted every alternate Saturday in the Sunday School Room. 12 participants regularly attended the programme which lasted for about 6 months. They were provided with the necessary printed lessons and were tested in the form of crossword quiz.

Contribution by Youth for Christ

We will be failing in our responsibilities if we do not mention the great support received from Trans-Yamuna Unit of Youth for Christ who also utilised the skilled members of CCN Youth Fellowship and other members of CCN Congregation and contributed a lot in the life & Ministry of the CCN. They were on 'call', so to speak, planning, preaching, supplying resource persons, besides conducting Praise & Worship along with CCN Youth, during VBS right from the first day of VBS. The CCN Youth Fellowship enjoyed the joint efforts, time and again, with Youth for Christ. The CCN Youth along with the Congregation expresses both appreciation & gratitude to the Director of Trans-Yamuna Unit of Youth for Christ Mr. Immanuel Joseph and his wife Mrs. Preeti Joseph for their leadership & contribution during this venture.

Church Choir

Rev. Kamal Mall and Mr. Rabindran Sunder Singh as the Choir Master revived the church choir, which was in disarray, due to various reasons. Since then the choir has done very well till date.

Bifurcation of Church Services

With the growing number of worshippers both in Hindi and in English segments, Rev. Kamal Mall, after obtaining the consent of the PC and the General Body, bifurcated the morning service into Hindi service, to begin at 08:00 a.m. and English Service, to begin at 09:45 AM. on Sundays. He made sure that the congregation stayed united by ensuring single Pastorate Committee for both these services and conducting Combined Service on the last Sunday of every month and on all occasions and festivals. The practice of conducting the Service by the members of Senior Members, Women, Youth, Sunday School Children on the fifth Sundays, in rotation continued.

Evening Praise and Worship Service

Rev. Kamal Mall also introduced Eucharist on all third Sundays of the Month during the evening Praise and Worship Service which resulted in the increase in the number of participants.

Sunday Evening Praise and Worship are being conducted, with the continued guidance and Pastoral oversight by Rev. Kamal Mal and Rev. Lomesh Chand, and presently Rev. Sunil Ghazan, with the active and dedicated support and participation of Mr. Ronald Das, Mrs. Roma Das, Dr. Mrs. Leila Varkey, Ms. Stella Miller, Mr. Immanuel Joseph, Mrs. Preeti Joseph, Mrs. Veena Wesley and Col. M.L. Lukose. Average attendance during the evening service stands at about 50 worshippers, including University students and those from other faiths.

Wednesday Prayer Cell

Wednesday Prayer meetings in the Church continued to be held under the able guidance of Rev. Lomesh Chand, co-Presbyter and Pastor in-charge of Greater Noida Parish, and now Rev. Sunil Ghazan. Mrs. Rita Gill took an active part in leading the Wednesday evening prayers especially when the Priest was not available. Over 60 people, including those from other faiths, attend this prayer session every week.

Dedicated Sunday's and Events

Defence Sunday

CCN dedicated one Sunday as 'Defence Sunday' by the Services veterans, who are members of the church, coordinated by Brig. Rajiv Williams, in February 2016. All the retired defence service officers take part in the organisation of the events of the Sunday and participate proudly displaying their decorations. The Pipers and Naval Band playing the favourite hymns, arranged by kind courtesy of the Former Chief of Naval Staff, Admiral Sushil Kumar, a member of our church enchanted the people. Defence Sunday was celebrated for the second time in November 2018 as part of the Thirty-Year celebration of the establishment of the Church. It has been suggested that this be made an annual feature in November first week every year.

Special Services

Sunday Services dedicated to 'Tribal and Adivasis', Bible Sundays, Leprosy Sundays etc. are being celebrated. Seminars and workshops on Christian themes are a regular feature. During Easter, Christmas and New Year, CCN conducts Midnight and Sun Rise services. On Maundy Thursdays, the Church conducts Feet Washing and Love Feast Services and on Good Fridays, three-hour Mid-Day Services are conducted ever since the time of Rev. Paul Swarup. Lenten Prayer Meetings are held at various homes by various Church group members during the Lenten Season.

WFCS

WFCS witnessed a renewed vigour under the leadership of Mrs Veena Wesley as its President. They are an active part of Diocesan WFCS Several activities were introduced and WFCS participated and helped in all the events of the church. She was instrumental in implementing the concept of 'Handful of Rice' as conceptualised by Mrs Thapliyal. They support two children from a Home in Jangpura and visit old age Homes once/twice every year. WFCS now manage their accounts and their savings has shown a steep increase.

Spiritual, Mission and Missionary Support

Rev. Kamal Mall continued to support those pursuing theological studies at renowned seminaries, instituted by Rev. Dr. Paul Swarup. He also extended financial support to two evangelical workers, one of CNI sponsored and the other IEM sponsored. Rev. Kamal Mall believed in supporting other churches and people in need of finances and in extending financial support to the Diocese of Delhi. Churches at Khekra & Barot have been recipients of this largesse, apart from Greater Noida.

CCN diligently supported children of the parish needing financial support for education and members and staff requiring medical treatment.

Greater Noida Christ Church

During the tenure of Rev. Kamal Mall, ably helped by Dn. Varun and Dn. Sachin and Rev. Lomesh Chand, CCGN saw exponential growth. Divine Services are being conducted at the Chapel of St. Thomas B. Ed. College, in Knowledge Park III, in Greater Noida, with the kind permission accorded by Rt. Rev. Sunil Singh, Bishop of Diocese of Delhi, CNI and continued support of Bishop Waris Masih, the current Bishop. About 18 families and around 60 individual worshippers regularly attended the Divine Service under the Pastoral care of Rev. Lomesh Chand. Initial incubation was under the able guidance of Rev. Dr. Paul Swarup and subsequently by Rev. Kamal Mall, who took it as a serious mission, and now being taken forward by Rev. Sunil Ghazan.

Positions of Pride

It is a matter of great pride for CCN that under the leadership of Rev. Kamal Mall, several members of our church were elected to the Diocesan Bodies. These are Rear Admiral Ramsay, Diocesan Executive Council, Mr. Victor Franklin- Finance Committee, Brig. R.E. Williams- Stewardship Committee, Mr. Prateek Jaswant – Law & Procedure, Dr. Mrs. Leila Varkey- Christian Life and Evangelism and Dr. Mrs. Helen Sekar –Court of the Diocese. It is notwithstanding the fact that our Priest was also the Treasurer of the Diocese.

Infrastructure and Other Implementations

Rev. Kamal Mall as the Treasurer of the Diocese of Delhi ensured the revival of integration of our annual accounts with that of the Diocesan Society, a long pending request to various Bishops.

The PA system was replaced with a modern system for quality of sound reproduction through the relentless efforts of Mr. Victor Franklin (who was two-term Hon. Secretary) and Mr. Shibu George and Mr. Prateek Jaswant, the Hon. Treasurers with Mr. Victor Franklin

This team was instrumental in the landfill and re-construction of rear wall projects. Needless to mention here that Wg. Cdr. Ransford Cowasjee, in-charge of Church maintenance supervised the work under difficult climatic conditions.

Wg. Cdr. Ransford Cowasjee also conceived separation of the electric connection of the main Church building and the Multi-Utility Complex. He made sure that this was fully executed despite the delays at the Noida Electricity Board.

During his term as the Hon. Secretary, Mr. Victor Franklin, duly supported by Mr. Anand Peter, Mr. Shibu George and Mr. Prateek Jaswant respectively as the Hon. Treasurers during their tenure, mooted the idea of further strengthening the accounts, administration and projects framework of the church by bringing out an SOP in the form of a handbook on 'Policies & Procedure', approved by the PC. They were wholeheartedly supported by Rev. Kamal Mall. Mr. Franklin sought the help of Mr. Peter who functioned as the Editor and producer of the handbook. Others who contributed were Brig. Williams, Mrs. Veena Wesley, Ms. Michele, Wg. Commander Ransford Cowasjee, Mrs. Kamna Cowasjee and Mrs. Christy Franklin. The handbook was duly received in the AGM and sent to PC for implementation. The implementation has since been done by the efforts of our 4th and current Presbyter-in-charge Rev. Sunil Solomon Ghazan in September 2018.

Air-conditioning of the main church building was another major project undertaken by the Hon. Secretary and Hon. Treasurer duo, Mr. Victor Franklin and Mr. Prateek Jaswant with the unwavering support of the Presbyter-in-Charge, Rev. Kamal Mall. This project was successfully executed.

Maintenance Committee

Though a committee was formed by the Pastorate Committee, it was virtually a one-man show by Wg. Cdr. Ransford Cowasjee, then a two-term member of the PC. All projects and tasks assigned to the committee were executed under his able supervision. He visited the church almost daily to monitor the work even when the weather was not favourable. At time of printing the committee comprises Col. P.D. Shah, Mr. Jeremiah Jayababu, Mrs. Veena

Wesley. The committee is looking after the maintenance work of the church, under the provisions of the AGM approved 'Policies & Procedure of CCN'.

Church Administrator

Mrs. Christy Franklin, an MCA and dedicated member of our church was inducted as the Church Administrator by Rev. Dr. Paul Swarup in the year 2009. She was trained by Mr. Peter in the maintenance of church accounts on Tally. He continues to mentor her and help her prepare quarterly accounts and annual audits under the supervision of the Hon. Treasurer, Mr. Prateek Jaswant. Rev. Kamal Mall mentored Mrs. Christy on other administrative matters. Mrs. Christy handles the Church office and outreach and willingly accepts additional responsibilities, especially during VBS, Fete and various festival seasons. She is an asset to CCN.

Transfer of Rev. Kamal Mall

On transfer, Rev. Kamal Mall, after an eventful period of 7 years, handed over charge of the church to Rev. Sunil Solomon Ghazan, our 4th Presbyter-in-charge. CCN and various entities in the church gave Rev. Kamal Mall and his family a grand farewell. The farewell function organised by the Church was well attended. Members spoke of the great work done by Rev. Kamal Mall and the unforgettable contribution of his wife Mrs. Neeta Mall and their very active daughters, Minhael and Michelle during family retreats, VBS and Youth Programmes. Rev. Kamal Mall with his dedication and innovative approach will join the 'Hall of Fame' of CCN along with Rev. Col. Lawrence Massey and Rev. Dr. Paul Swarup.

July 2018 – November 2018
30th Anniversary of the Church

The New Shepherd

Rev. Sunil Solomon Ghazan took charge from Rev. Kamal Mall on the 17th June 2018. Rev. Ghazan is a visionary and is guiding the Church spiritually. Being in the transition period, he had the opportunity to take part and bless the children of VBS 2018, held at Somerville International School, and at the Grand Finale held at CCN on 24 June2018, by the Church, under the leadership of Rev. and Mrs. Mall.

We look up to him for our spiritual growth and peace. Since he took charge he is leading and guiding the congregation for "Happy Living" through the WhatsApp Group he has created, the message he disseminates through Weekly Flier, his sermons on Sunday worship, and his special sermon to commemorate the establishment of CCN on its 30th anniversary. He is a believer in preserving Church history and a great supporter in bringing out this booklet

Ministry of Rev. Sunil Solomon Ghazan

Since he took over as Pastor-in-Charge Rev. Ghazan commenced visiting families and the sick. He believes in being a hands-on pastor and is available to the parishioners 24×7. Mrs. Saroj Solomon Gazan, his wife, is a silent support, and very accommodative and hosted a 'Thanksgiving Service and Dinner' to the Parishioners on Friday the 8th August 2018, on her birthday. She regularly attends the morning Hindi service and exhibits great enthusiasm and interacts with the parishioners.

Office for the Pastor

In order to have regular contact and interaction with the parishioners, Rev. Sunil Ghazan, on his joining CCN, organized an 'Office of the Pastor-in-Charge' on the ground floor of the Multi Utility Complex, dividing the Sunday School hall into two parts. The office was dedicated by Bishop Santram and declared open on 19th August 2018, after the Divine Service, a veritable proof of his availability.

Independence Day 2018

Independence Day was celebrated on the 15th of August 2018, in a special and befitting manner, with a Praise and Worship Service in the Church, followed by the 'National Flag Hoisting' in the Lawns of the Church. Children of our Outreach Project participated with great enthusiasm in the event and performed on the occasion. Sweets were distributed. Rev. Sunil Ghazan invited Brig. Rajiv Williams to hoist the National Flag. The function was well attended, including Senior Defence Services veterans of the Church. At the time of writing, the Church had a flag-hoisting ceremony on 26 January with Rev. Col. Lawrence Massey hoisting the flag.

Kerala Flood Relief

CCN organised a Special Sunday Service on 26 August 2018 as the 'Kerala Flood Relief Funds Collection Programme' and sent the proceeds to the Diocese of Delhi for onward delivery to the Flood-Stricken Kerala through CSI. Service was conducted by the Youth Group, while the celebrant was Rev. Sunil Gazan.

WFCS, under the leadership of Dr. Mrs. Lucky Chandekar and Mrs. Veena Wesley had organised a Flood Relief Programme and on two instalments sent essential medicines, through Indian Air Force aircraft on relief duty and subsequently through a Relief Train organised by the Bar Association of Supreme Court of India, in response to a call from Hon'ble Justice Kurian on behalf of Kerala Christian Association in Delhi.

Tribal Sunday

CCN conducted a Special Service on 'Tribal Sunday' on 30th September 2018, during which Christians of Tribal Regions, now residing in Noida, actively participated, along with our members.

It may be noted that Tribes existed from Old Testament Era. One may recall the 12 Tribes of Israelites, descendants of 12 sons of Jacob as we see in Joshua 1: 12-13. Some Tribes became affluent, and some were not; some were strong, and some were weak. Sons of men in Old Testament Era were considered as arrows in the quiver of a soldier. Ps 127.

Confirmation Classes

Confirmation classes for the year 2018-19 for both Adults and Youth have commenced after the Divine Service from 21st October 2018, by Rev. Solomon Ghazan. Participants were free to interact with the Pastor and asked questions on observing 'Local Traditions' in a modern Christian environment; especially the obligations of those recently converted from other faiths to Christianity.

NCWA Events

Rev. Ghazan has shown great interest in unity - Programmes of NCWA, with a view to revive our participation.

NCWA inter denominational Children's Festival, for the current year, was conducted in our Church on the 13th October 2018. Thanks to the organisers, Mrs. Preeti Joseph, Dr. Lucky Chandekar, Mr. Joseph Immanuel, Youth Group, Elders, and the Pastorate Committee Members.

As mentioned elsewhere, CCN had played important role in the functioning of NCWA. Mr Abraham Daniel is the present General Secretary of NCWA and has been instrumental in organising the Children's festival.

As part of the NCWA Christmas Programme and Christmas Float, which could not be conducted due to political turmoil in the state, we conducted an Ecumenical Worship Service of all the Major Member Churches of NCWA on the 16 December 2018, in our Church.

Defence Sunday

4th November 2018 was observed as Defence Sunday under the aegis of Senior Member Fellowship. Service was in two parts: usual Divine Service followed by a Remembrance Day Ritual. Thanks to Brig Rajiv Williams and the Defence Personnel of the Church for the efficient planning and conduct of all the events of the day.

Sports Festival

Sports festival to commemorate the 30 Years of Spiritual Journey, under the able leadership of Mr. Jeremiah Jai Babu, Mr. Alwyn Theodore and the Youth Group, was also held from 28 October to 4th Nov 2018 for Children, both boys and girls of age groups from 6-10 years and for common groups of women and men. Winners were felicitated.

Greater Noida Extension of the Church

Rev. Sunil Gazan, presently, takes care of the spiritual needs of CCGN also, due to the transfer of Rev. Lomesh Chand. Both CCN and CCGN have great hopes and expectations from Rev. Sunil Solomon Ghazan in maintaining the tempo of development created by his predecessors Rev. Dr. Paul Swarup and Rev. Kamal Mall.

30th Anniversary of the Church and Garden Fete

As usual the Anniversary celebrations with the Garden Fete was celebrated with Full Gusto on the Sunday the 11th November. Apart from the Chief Guest Mr. Thomas T Roy, Secretary cum Treasurer of Lott Carrey Baptist Mission, we were happy to honour Rev Col Lawrence Massey, the Founder Priest, as a Guest of Honour, a unique treat by the Present Priest in Charge. The Fete was blessed by the Bishop of Delhi Diocese, Rt. Rev Warris Masih.

In addition, the actual 30th Anniversary Thanksgiving Eucharist Service was conducted on 13 November 2018 with Cakes and Refreshments.

Christmas 2018 and New year 2019

Christmas 2018 was celebrated with much pomp and show and greater devotion. Carol Rounds, Candlelight Service combined with nine lessons and Carol, Christmas Tree, Christmas play by Youth and Sunday School children and the Hearining Impaired Fellowship followed by Bonfire and Christmas Dinner was rather Unique. Chalera Outreach Under privileged Children Programmes also dominated the Festival.

Carols around Bonfire with Potluck Dinner hosted by the Priest In Charge was an additional feature, enjoyed by many.

Christmas Midnight and Morning Eucharist service were attended by many including People from other faith. A meaningful Crib with an Electronic Controlled Santa Claus added to the Show. Non-Christians thronged the Church, its lawn and the road till about 10 p.m. and the visitors were briefed and controlled by the dedicated Teams under Mrs. Vineeta Williams. The Programme culminated with Watch-night Midnight and Covenant Eucharist Services of the New Year, all of which were well attended by the Congregation.

St. Paul wrote:

"I planted, Apollos watered, but God gave the increase. So, neither he who plants nor he who waters is anything, but only God gives the growth."

1 Corinthians Ch, 3: v 6 & 7.

9 789388 945462